Living Green

Picking Up Trash

By Meg Gaertner

level 2 little blue readers

www.littlebluehousebooks.com

Little Blue House is distributed by North Star Editions:
sales@northstareditions.com | 888-417-0195

Produced for Little Blue House by Red Line Editorial.

Photographs ©: Shutterstock Images, cover, 4, 7, 8–9, 10, 16, 19, 20–21, 23, 24 (top left), 24 (top right), 24 (bottom left), 24 (bottom right); iStockphoto, 13, 14–15

Library of Congress Control Number: 2022901944

ISBN
978-1-64619-595-4 (hardcover)
978-1-64619-622-7 (paperback)
978-1-64619-673-9 (ebook pdf)
978-1-64619-649-4 (hosted ebook)

Printed in the United States of America
Mankato, MN
082022

About the Author

Meg Gaertner enjoys reading, writing, dancing, and being outside. She lives in Minnesota.

Table of Contents

trash

Picking Up Trash

A boy sees trash outside.

The trash is on the ground.

The boy puts on gloves.

He picks up the trash.

glove

The boy throws the
trash away.
He puts it in a trash can.

animal
trash

Helping Animals

Trash can hurt animals.

Animals might eat it.

They might become sick.

Trash can trap animals.

Animals might get stuck.

animal
trash

Picking up trash
helps animals.
It keeps them safe.

Keeping Earth Clean

You can plan a cleanup

to help Earth.

Invite your family and friends.

Trash can carry germs.

Wear gloves to stay safe.

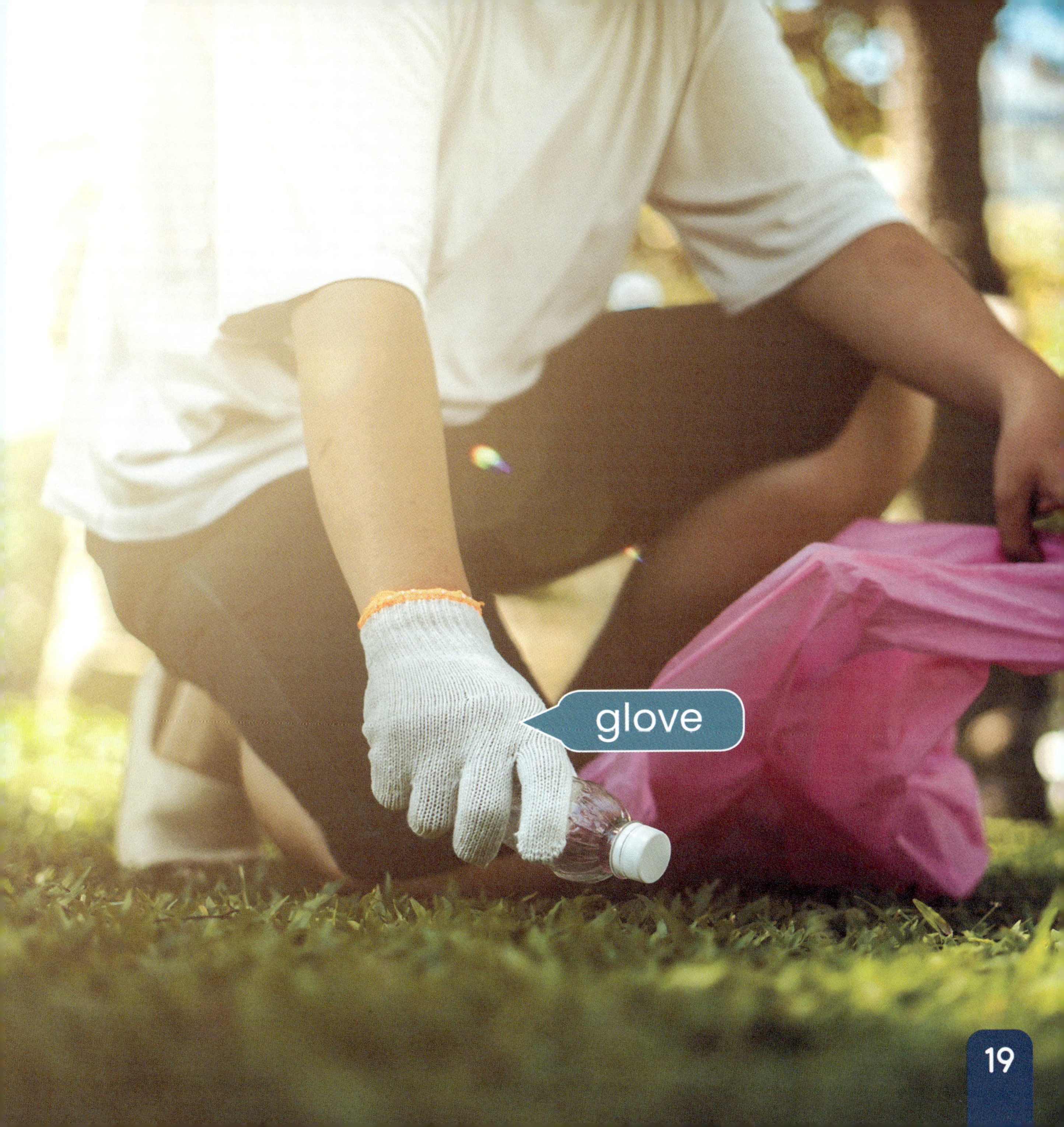
glove

Walk around outside.

Pick up trash.

Throw it in a trash can.

Or bring a trash bag.

trash bag

Picking up trash
helps Earth.
You can keep Earth clean.

Glossary

glove

trash bag

trash

trash can

Index